Harry didn't say anything, but he listened
and watched.

3

"I'm glad that hairy monster can't come on holiday with us," said Charlie. "Don't think of hiding him – because I'm watching." Charlie was Clare's brother and he was scared of spiders.

Clare did think about hiding Harry, but decided against it. She knew she would miss him a lot – and he would miss her. But she didn't want him to get into trouble.

Harry the Clever Spider
on holiday

Written by Julia Jarman
Illustrated by Charlie Fowkes

Harry was Clare's pet spider and he was very clever. Clare wanted to take Harry on holiday to Spain, but Mum said she couldn't.

"We need him to stay at home to keep an eye on things," Mum explained. "Besides, animals aren't allowed on planes."

"Harry isn't an animal!" cried Clare. "He's a minibeast."

She helped her mum put address labels on the cases.

"We don't want to lose them," Dad said. "We'll need our swimsuits for the beach."

"And we don't want to lose the necklace Dad's going to buy me for my birthday from a shop at the airport!" said Mum, excitedly.

Clare felt sad driving to the airport without Harry.

Then when they were in the check-in queue she felt something tickling her hand. She guessed who. Oh no! Naughty Harry!

"What are you laughing at?" said Charlie suspiciously.

"Nothing," said Clare. "Why don't you keep an eye on your things? Someone might take a fancy to your computer game."

But Charlie put his game away and kept a lookout for Harry.

When they were on the plane, Clare headed for the toilets as soon as she could. "You've got to keep hidden," she told Harry sternly.

But Harry tickled her again on the way back to her seat and she bumped into a man.
"Stop it," she whispered crossly.

"Who were you talking to?" asked Charlie.

"No one," said Clare. "Why don't we play I-spy?"

"Because I'd rather spy on you," said Charlie.

Luckily, Harry stayed in Clare's pocket until they reached their hotel. But then he came up for air and Charlie spotted him.

"MUM! DAD! CLARE'S BROUGHT HER HORRIBLE HAIRY SPIDER ON HOLIDAY!"

Charlie started bawling. Mum started calming him down. Dad started telling Clare off.

Clare was very upset. Mum and Dad were cross with her and Harry had completely disappeared.

Clare started to look for Harry and noticed that one of their cases was missing. "Mum! Dad!"

"What is it now?" said Dad, who was checking in. Mum was still comforting Charlie.

Clare pointed to the empty space where Mum's case had been – and suddenly noticed a trail of thread. Extra-special thick spider thread!

"Come on, Dad! Someone's stolen Mum's case, but Harry's on to it!"

Clare ran as fast as she could, weaving in and out of holiday-makers, following the thread. Dad was close behind and as they reached the door they saw a woman with Mum's case. She was getting into the back of a taxi where a man was waiting impatiently.

"STOP THIEF!" Clare shouted as loud as she could, but the taxi door slammed shut.

"Get going!" the woman inside screeched. "Start the car!"

Where was Harry? Was he in the taxi too?
Clever Harry! Clare realised he had been trying to
warn her all along. Perhaps he had overheard
the pair plotting. But now Harry was in danger.
If the thieving pair got away she might never see
him again.

"Too late!' yelled Dad.

But the taxi wasn't moving. The driver hadn't even started it. Why not?

Clare was very worried about Harry. She peered into the car. The man and woman were both yelling at the driver, who looked terrified. Clare saw why. Harry was on the steering wheel, looking very fierce.

"Start the car!" The man shook his fist at the driver, but he couldn't move. He couldn't turn the ignition key which was wrapped round with black spider thread.

"Hurray for Harry!" said Clare as the police took
the robbers away. "Hurray for Harry the Clever Spider!"

Everyone – even Charlie – agreed that Harry was a very clever spider.

"A useful one too," said Mum. "We'll always bring him on holiday now."

"Yippee!" shouted Clare as they all headed for the sea.

Harry just smiled proudly.

Harry can help!

Have you had something stolen?

Call Harry on : 88881 43567
or email Harry at harryspider@web.net

Harry can find it for you!

What Harry can do

Harry can tickle.

Harry can make a trail.

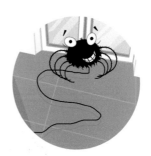

Harry can stop thieves.

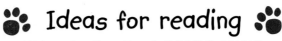

Ideas for reading

Written by Clare Dowdall BA(Ed), MA(Ed)
Lecturer and Primary Literacy Consultant

Learning objectives: know how to tackle unfamiliar words that are not completely decodable; give some reasons why things happen or characters change; engage with books through exploring and enacting interpretations; speak with clarity and use appropriate intonation when reading aloud

Curriculum links: Citizenship: Choices

Interest words: suitcase, minibeast, necklace, queue, suspiciously, sternly, bawling, comforting, weaving, ignition, proudly

Word count: 702

Resources: ICT, whiteboard

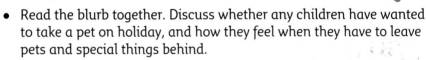

Getting started

- Read the blurb together. Discuss whether any children have wanted to take a pet on holiday, and how they feel when they have to leave pets and special things behind.

- Ask children to predict how Harry will save the day and give reasons for their ideas, making notes on the whiteboard.

- Look at the interest words list. Discuss how many words are made from smaller words and familiar parts. Remind children to use this along with phonics as a strategy to read unfamiliar words.

Reading and responding

- Read pp2–3 together aloud. Model and discuss how to use expression to bring the characters to life through reading aloud.

- Focus on the character of Harry. Ask children to suggest how Harry might be feeling when he hears he's being left behind.

- Ask children to read aloud to the end of the story, focusing on using expression for speech.

- Support children as they read, helping them to use punctuation to develop expression.